For everyone who makes the world a little

brighter!

Truependous Publishing
Text Copyright © 2022 Laura Truepenny & Ben Humphreys
Illustrations Copyright © 2022 Hazel Narbett
ISBN: 978-1-7397845-1-5 (PB)

BOB on the Road to

Enlightenment

Written by Laura Truepenny and Ben Humphreys

Illustrated by Hazel Narbett

Truependous Publishing

Meet Bob.

Bob is a campervan.

A bright orange, shiny campervan.

The funny thing is, he didn't start off this way.

This is his story.

It all began in the van factory on a stormy day.
The machines were adding the finishing touches to all the vans...

...when something very UNEXPECTED happened!

A lightning bolt tore a hole in the factory roof and a dazzling rainbow shone through.

Bob was struck with

powerful RAINBOW MAGIC!

It turned him orange - bright orange!

It also did something else...

Something to his inner workings...

Something magical...

Something mystifying!

Bob left the factory for the first time feeling **incredible!**

Parking up outside, he admired his reflection in the windows.

With his sleek black tyres,

gleaming paintwork

and shiny silver badge,

Bob thought he looked

fantastic.

Just then, a campervan named Graham pulled up next to him.
Tearing himself away from his reflection, Bob turned to look.

"I'm so much more colourful than you!"
he said with a smirk.

At that moment, the needle
on Bob's fuel gauge started to quiver.

He didn't notice, but it went down!

Graham recognised Bob instantly and replied,
"Yes, I heard about the incident with the rai bow!
You might be orange now, but we are still the same."

"How are we the same?" Bob asked, feeling puzzled.

"We both have an engine and four wheels - in this world, there are many vans of many colours. One colour is not better than another, it's just different."

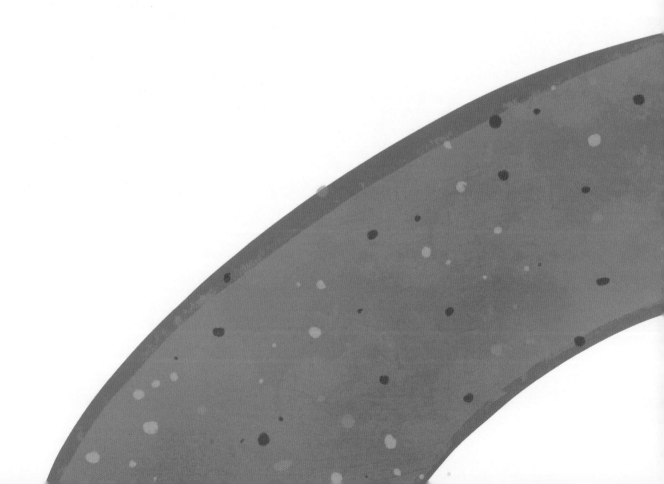

Graham certainly made a good point, but Bob didn't have
time to think about that - he was too excited to go exploring!

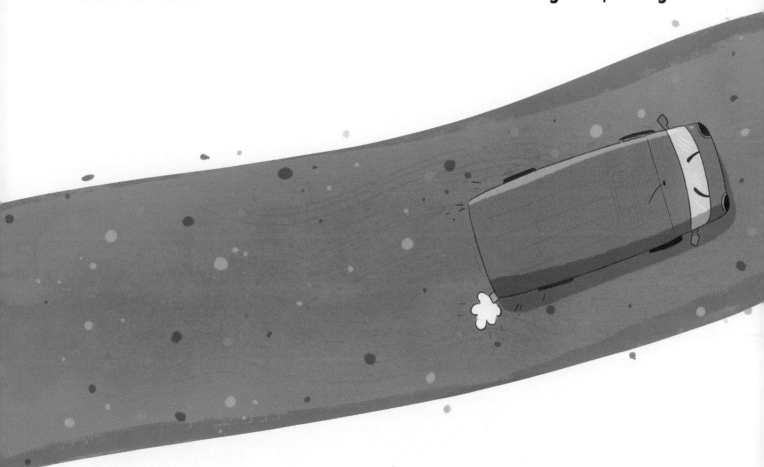

He **revved** his engine, **flashed** his lights and **embarked** on
his very first journey...

As he was driving along, he spotted a dented, rather muddy campervan named Ethel in the supermarket car park.

He drove closer...

and closer...

until he was right next to her.

"I'm shinier than you!" Bob teased.

Ethel looked at Bob with a kind smile on her face.

"True beauty comes from within, Bob. It's what's inside that counts," she said.

Bob wasn't quite sure what Ethel meant.
Feeling perplexed, he decided to continue driving.

A few miles down the road, he parked up at a
spot with breathtaking views of the countryside.

Another campervan was already there.

"Wow, you look old and rusty. I bet I can drive faster than you!"
Bob said.

Rusty raised his eyebrow a little, an amused look on his face.

"Come on, let's have a race, Rusty!" said Bob,
"Last one to Travellers' Rest is a rotten egg!"

Bob sped off on
to the motorway,
confident that he
would win.

Rusty rattled slowly
down the country lanes.

Half an hour later, Bob arrived
at Travellers' Rest.

"Yes! I knew I would be the fastest!"
he smiled to himself.

Some time later, Rusty turned up.

"I beat you!" Bob said joyously.

"Yes you did, but I saw some spectacular sights on my drive!" Rusty said. "It's not always about getting somewhere the fastest, Bob."

Bob paused in the shadow of the mountains and felt very small for a moment. He hadn't seen anything of interest on his journey.

Feeling deflated, he decided to go for a drive along the country lanes, with Rusty's words echoing in his mind.

All of a sudden, Bob's engine started to judder.
Panicking, he noticed his fuel gauge was glowing red.

His tank had been full at the start of his journey, and now it was
nearly empty! He hadn't driven that far!

What could be happening?

He juddered into a layby and ground to a halt.

Just then, a flashy new motorhome named Greta arrived and jeered at Bob, "Bright green is so much better than orange!"

Bob thought back to his conversation with Graham.

"You might be green, but we're quite similar really. We both have an engine and four wheels. One colour is not better than another, it's just different."

The needle on Bob's fuel gauge suddenly sprang to life and glowed with **rainbow magic**!

Then, slowly but surely, it appeared to fill up a little!

Greta added, "Well, I'm so much shinier than you!"

Bob remembered Ethel's words of wisdom
from his trip to the supermarket.

"True beauty comes from within," he said.

Yet again, the needle moved -
his tank was filling up even more!

Greta, feeling perplexed, searched her mind for something else
she could say: "Well...well... I bet I am much faster than you!"

An image of Rusty entered Bob's mind. He smiled.

"It's not always about being the fastest. It's about what you see and who you meet along the way."

Bob was delighted to see that his fuel gauge
was no longer glowing red.

In fact, his tank was almost full to the brim!

With a new lease of life, he drove away through the countryside,
leaving Greta lost for words.

Just down the road, Bob caught a glimpse of some campervans he recognised. He pulled up in front of them.

"You've all taught me some truly valuable lessons," Bob said. "Fancy going for a drive together?"

Rusty, Ethel and Graham laughed joyously.
"Why of course. Where shall we go?" they asked.

Bob thought for a moment.
"I don't mind, as long as we take the scenic route!"

Bob is a campervan.

A muddier, wiser campervan,
continuing on the
Road to Enlightenment!

How can you fill your own fuel tank?

Be kind to yourself and others

Give compliments

Practise good manners

Appreciate the little things

Take the scenic route!

Meet the Real Bob!

Bob (also known as the Big Orange Beast) left the VW factory for the first time in October 2018, and lived in Germany for over a year. During his time there, he enjoyed many trips exploring Europe.

In January 2020, he went on an epic three-month tour through France, Spain and Portugal. It was when Bob was driving through Portugal that his friends Laura and Ben wrote the story
Bob on the Road to Enlightenment!

Since then, Bob has been on many road trips, and lots of weekend trips here, there and everywhere. He particularly loves festivals. Bob resides in a wonderful town called Bideford in North Devon.

Meet the Authors!

Laura Truepenny is a qualified primary school teacher, and taught in British schools in Germany for seven years. These days, she is a mum, childminder and tutor. She is at her absolute happiest when at a festival, covered in glitter and dancing around with her family and friends.

Ben Humphreys is a qualified secondary science teacher and was head of biology for several years, also in Germany. He loves being outdoors: camping, mountain-biking and hunting for Pokemon! As well as being a busy dad, he is a childminder to lots of Truependous Tots!

Ben and Laura both practise Nichiren Buddhism, which cherishes all individuals as unique beings, who have the ability to contribute to the world in a positive way. Nichiren Buddhists hold the view that everyone is important, should be valued, and has the innate potential to reach enlightenment in this lifetime. Their practice inspired the concept of Bob on the Road to Englightenment.

Nam-Myoho-Renge-Kyo!

Meet the illustrator!

Hazel Narbett is an illustrator and mum to two wild children, who she home educates. She loves animals (especially goats) and has a dog, rats and two axolotls. She enjoys spending time outside and exploring nature with her family. Some of her favourite things are baths, naps and food!